SABAN'S

MIGHTY MORPHIN
POWER RANGERS
™

THE SUPER ZORDS!

By Jean Waricha

A PARACHUTE PRESS BOOK

A PARACHUTE PRESS BOOK
Parachute Press, Inc.
156 Fifth Avenue
New York, NY 10010

Creative Consultant: Cheryl Saban.

With special thanks to Cheryl Saban, Debi Young, Ban Pryor, and
Sherry Stack.

Printed in the U.S.A.
August 1994
ISBN: 0-938753-87-8
B C D E F G H I J

PROLOGUE

Evil forces beware. Six ordinary teenagers are about to morph into—the Mighty Morphin Power Rangers.

Jason, Kimberly, Trini, Zack, and Billy received their incredible powers from Zordon, a good wizard trapped in another dimension. Zordon gave each teenager a magic coin—a Power Morpher— and super strength drawn from the spirits of the dinosaurs.

It was different for Tommy. He received his incredible power from the evil Rita Repulsa, who found one of Zordon's magic coins. She gave it to Tommy and tricked him into helping her carry out her wicked deeds. But once he met the Power Rangers, he was convinced to use his power to fight the forces of Evil.

Sometimes the forces of Evil prove too strong for even the Power Rangers' super strength! So when things get really tough, the Power Rangers call upon their

Dinozords—giant robots they drive into battle.

Power Rangers, dinosaur spirits, and amazing robots—together these incredible forces protect the Earth.

So—get ready. *It's morphin time!*

CHAPTER 1

"Let me hear you say, 'Go!' Go! That's right! Let me hear you say, 'Fight!' Fight! All right!"

The cheers of seven junior high school girls echoed in the Angel Grove Youth Center gym. They were practicing for cheerleader tryouts. With each cheer, the girls jumped up in the air and shook their red and white pom-poms wildly.

Kimberly and her good friend Tommy sat in the bleachers, watching. Kimberly hoped that all the girls would make the team. But she was really rooting for one red-headed, freckle-faced girl, her twelve-year-old cousin, Kelly. She'd be especially proud if Kelly made it!

"I think it's really cool that Kelly wants to be a cheerleader like you," said Tommy, flashing a smile.

"Kelly's been working hard," said Kimberly, brushing a strand of her shoulder-length, light brown hair from her eyes. "But sometimes, when she makes a mistake, she loses her confidence."

Kimberly and Tommy both knew how important it was to be confident. Kimberly and Tommy and their best friends Jason, Trini, Billy, and Zack shared an amazing secret. Whenever danger threatened the Earth, they changed— into the Mighty Morphin Power Rangers! Together they used their secret superpowers and incredible confidence to protect the planet from evil forces.

Tommy hadn't always been a Power Ranger, though. In the past, the dark-haired teen with the ponytail had been lured by

Rita Repulsa to carry out her evil deeds. But once he'd met the Power Rangers, he was convinced that he should use his strength for Good. That's when he became a Power Ranger himself.

"Kelly looks great out there today," Kimberly added.

"She looks awesome," Tommy agreed. "I'm *sure* she'll make the team."

Kimberly and Tommy watched as the cheerleading coach had the girls form a perfectly straight line. When all eyes were on them, the coach shouted, "Ready team, go!"

Together the girls leaped to the left. Then they jumped to the right, cheering in loud voices.

Everyone stayed in step—well, almost everyone. Kelly missed a beat and soon found herself leaping while the other girls were landing.

Almost in tears, Kelly stopped cheering and shuffled her way over to the bleachers.

"Kelly," said Kimberly, "what's wrong? Why did you stop?"

"It's no use," Kelly answered with her head hanging down. "I'm never going to make the cheerleading squad. I can't do anything right. I look so stupid out there."

Kimberly hugged Kelly. Then she said firmly, "Don't worry. You and I can practice the routine together. I'll help you."

"It's too late to practice," Kelly told Kimberly. "Tryouts are later today. I'll never get the cheer right in time."

"Let's try it together," said Kimberly. She took her cousin by the hand and led her off to the other end of the gym. "Just watch me."

Kelly sat cross-legged on the floor and studied Kimberly smoothly performing the cheer. Kimberly was a great gymnast— each of her moves was perfect.

"Wow!" said Kelly. "You are *so* good."

"Thanks," said Kimberly. "But it just takes practice, that's all. Why don't you give it a try now?"

"I don't know," Kelly replied, her voice full of doubt. But she slowly climbed to her feet and took her place beside her cousin.

Kelly and Kimberly were completely unaware that someone was spying on them. Someone miles and miles away from Earth. Someone who was up to no good. She was the evil Rita Repulsa, and from her gloomy fortress on the moon, she was watching every move the girls made.

Rita clutched her magic telescope with her long, pointed fingernails. Rita loved pointy things. The sleeves and collar of her gown hung down in sharp points. And on her head, she wore a crown of two pointed cones.

"You slimy teenagers should be cheering for me!" screeched Rita in a voice that could shatter glass. *"Me! Me! Me!"*

"We'll cheer for you, O Queen of Badness," said Baboo and Squatt, two of Rita's dim-witted helpers. Baboo looked like a hideous monkey with bony black wings, while Squatt had an ugly blue face and crooked teeth that cried out for braces. Mostly, they bickered with each other or buttered up Rita, which is what they were doing now.

Baboo and Squatt waved their arms over their heads, swaying from side to side, and together they shouted, "Rita, Rita. She is fun. She repulses everyone."

"Oh, you two dears," Rita cooed, almost sweetly. "I love it when you flatter me with such sweet poetry."

But, as usual, Rita's good mood lasted only seconds.

"Finster," she shrieked, calling out the name of her chief monster-maker.

"Tell Finster I want a monster to finally finish off those Power Rangers," she ordered Baboo and Squatt. "Once they're gone, I'll make the whole Earth cheer—for Queen Rita!"

CHAPTER 2

Back on Earth, Kimberly and Kelly were still rehearsing cheers. But Kelly was getting worse instead of better. Finally she stopped and threw her pom-poms down.

"Oh, Kim," she cried. "I just can't get it right. Maybe I should drop out of the tryouts."

"No way," said Tommy, who was watching from the side.

"Don't give up," Kimberly pleaded. "We'll start over. Come on—give it another try."

Just then Angel Grove's two biggest troublemakers, Bulk and Skull, strolled into the gym. Bulk was a big guy with a greasy pony-tail. He liked to bully everyone, especially his buddy, Skull. Skull was a skinny guy with dirty black hair. He always dressed in black. Today, Bulk was wearing one of his usual disgusting outfits, a stained green shirt with a rubber vest and black gloves cut off at the fingers.

"Well, well, well," Bulk snickered. "What do we have here? Look Skull—a couple of wanna-be cheerleaders."

"Yeah. Rah-rah-rah," Skull said dully.

The two paraded over to Kelly. Bulk grabbed her pom-poms. "Catch," he said, tossing one over to Skull.

"Hey," shouted Kelly. She reached for the other pom-pom. Bulk waved it around, just above Kelly's head.

"Okay, guys, give Kelly back her pom-poms," said Tommy, coming to Kelly's aid. "She needs to practice for the tryouts."

"Sure, we'll give 'em back,"

sneered Bulk. "We'll even help her out. We'll show her a few new moves."

"Yeah," Skull added. "Let's show them our stuff, big guy."

Then Bulk and Skull pranced around the gym, shouting in high, squeaky voices. "Two-four-six-eight. Who should you appreci-ate? Bulk and Skull. Bulk and Skull. Yaaaay...Bulk and Skull!"

They finished the cheer by leaping high into the air. Then Skull tumbled to the floor, rolling in laughter at his own perfor-mance. But Bulk just stood there, frozen, with his arms still over his head and a look of incredible pain on his face.

"My back," gasped Bulk. "I can't move!"

"Just a sec," said Kimberly. She jumped up and grabbed the pom-pom from Bulk's stiff hand. "I don't think you'll be needing this anymore."

Tommy, Kimberly, and Kelly shook their heads as Skull helped Bulk limp out of the gym.

Far away on the moon, Rita was definitely *not* laughing. She glared at Goldar, her chief warrior, and Baboo and Squatt. Her lips twisted into an ugly sneer, and she shouted, "Finster, where's my monster, you dim-witted idiot?"

"Your new monster is in the

Monster-matic, Your Evilness. Have patience."

"It better be tough enough to destroy the Power Rangers," Goldar warned, his red eyes glinting. Goldar was always in a bad mood.

"Oh, don't worry," Finster said proudly. "This time I've created a frightening monster that will crush those Power Rangers for sure!" His ratlike gray face attempted a smile.

"Well, you'd better be sure! But what's taking so long?" Rita yelled, jabbing her pointy fingernails into Finster's shoulder.

"Your Great Awfulness," Goldar interrupted, "while we wait for

Finster's monster, why don't we send the Putty Patrol to capture Kimberly's little cousin Kelly? We will force her to cheer for you, O Queen of Badness."

"What a good idea," said Rita. "Something new for you."

She cackled in delight. Then, at the very top of her lungs, Rita screamed, "Putties! I want my Putties—now!"

While Rita screeched for her Putty Patrol, Jason, Billy, and Trini headed to the gym to meet their friends. Zack, dressed in black hi-tops and black and white striped pants, hip-hopped after them.

Ernie, who ran the snack bar at

the youth center, met them at the door. "Boy, am I glad to see you guys," he said.

"What's up?" Jason asked, running a hand through his short brown hair.

"My delivery truck broke down and I need someone to run downtown to pick up some supplies."

"No problem," said Jason, always willing to help out. "I'll go."

While Jason hurried to help Ernie, the other teenagers joined Kimberly, Tommy, and Kelly.

"Okay, Kelly, let's try it from the beginning," Kimberly suggested.

"How's she doing?" Trini whispered to Tommy as she tucked a

loose strand of long black hair back into her braid.

"She'll be fine if—" Before Tommy could finish, Kelly cried out, "Forget it. I just can't do it. I'll never be as good as you, Kimberly. Why should I even bother trying out for the team?" Then she ran out of the gym in tears.

"Hang tight," Tommy told Billy, Zack, and Trini. Then he and Kimberly sprinted outside after Kelly. They found her sitting on a swing, staring at the ground.

"Hey, is there room for two more out here?" Tommy asked.

"I guess," Kelly said.

Kimberly sat in the swing next

to her cousin and said, "Kel, you shouldn't compare yourself to me or anyone else. And you must never give up. Believe in yourself and you can do whatever you want."

"Come on, Kelly," Tommy urged. "Just give yourself another chance!"

While Kimberly, Tommy, and Kelly talked, several dark figures somersaulted through the air toward them. The creatures landed silently in the grass and quietly surrounded the three.

Suddenly Tommy looked up. "Putties!" he shouted in warning.

Kimberly quickly jumped to her feet. "Kelly," she cried,

"stay behind us!"

Tommy and Kimberly turned to face the Putties.

"Come on, clay-brains," said Tommy. That was all Rita's soldiers needed to hear. They attacked.

Kim neatly placed her fist in one Putty's stomach while Tommy dropped another to the ground with a spin kick.

Two more Putties took their place. Kimberly and Tommy jumped and dodged as they defended themselves. They fought so hard they lost track of Kelly. And they didn't notice Baboo and Squatt appear in a sudden flash of light.

Finally Kimberly and Tommy finished off the Putties.

"Good going!" said Tommy.

"But where's Kelly?" Kimberly asked, searching frantically.

They turned and spotted Baboo and Squatt sneaking up on Kelly. The evil twosome yanked her roughly by the arms.

"No!" yelled Kimberly. But it was too late. In an instant Kelly vanished along with Squatt and Baboo.

"We did it! We did it!" Baboo and Squatt squealed in delight. They had just reappeared with their prisoner in one of Rita's hidden caves on the moon. "Rita is going to be so proud of us."

As they jumped up and down with excitement, Kelly fearfully glanced around the smelly, dark cave. "What do you think you're doing with me?" she asked, trying to sound brave. "Why did you bring me here?"

"You'll find out soon enough," grunted Baboo.

Meanwhile, inside Rita's cold fortress, the evil queen was shrieking even louder than usual.

"I've waited long enough, Finster! I want my monster!"

Finster shot a nervous glance at the huge hourglass next to Rita. The last grains of sand trickled down from the top.

"At last it's ready, O Queen of Evilness!" said Finster. "Shall we go to my lab to see the monster before I send it to destroy Earth?"

Finster led the way. Slowly, they descended the slimy green stone steps to his hidden chamber. When they reached the bottom of the steps, the stench in the air was thick and foul.

"Oh, the new monster's done, all right," said Rita. "I can smell a done monster a mile away. And what a sweet smell it is."

Finster carefully opened the door to his smelly lab. "Meet the Lizzinator," he said proudly. Rita and Goldar were dazzled—the Lizzinator was the most hideous monster either of them had ever seen. And it was ready to destroy everything on Earth *and* the Power Rangers—once and for all!

CHAPTER 4

Kimberly and Tommy burst through the doors of the youth center gym, calling for Billy, Zack, and Trini to come quickly. They gathered in a huddle to make sure no one could hear them.

"Squatt and Baboo snatched Kelly," Kimberly said, her dark

eyes filled with worry. "We've got to get to the Command Center fast and talk to Zordon. He'll know what to do."

"Shouldn't we find Jason first and tell him what's going on?" Zack questioned.

"There's no time. Kelly's in big trouble," Tommy urged. "We've got to go now!"

A second later, the five friends vanished.

Downtown, Jason was carrying the heavy snack bar supplies out of the warehouse. Suddenly the ground trembled beneath him and the entire warehouse building started to shake.

"I'll never be a good cheerleader," Kelly says to Kimberly and Tommy.

The Putty Patrol sneaks up on Tommy, Kimberly, and Kelly!

Kimberly dodges a high Putty slam!

Ki-yaaah! Tommy cracks a Putty with a kick!

While Tommy and Kimberly fight off the Putties, Baboo and Squatt kidnap Kelly!

Kimberly is concerned about Kelly. "We've got to get to the Command Center fast and talk to Zordon!"

Alpha 5 learns all about Rita's latest monster—the Lizzinator!

In a flash, the six teenagers morph into— Power Rangers!

The Green Ranger is ready to crush the Lizzinator!

Meanwhile, in a secret cave, Baboo and Squatt squeal in delight as they clutch their prisoner!

Kelly's escape plan has Baboo and Squatt dizzy with cheers!

It was a great day for the Pink Ranger—she helped destroy the Lizzinator and rescue Kelly!

"What's going on?" Jason said aloud as boxes came tumbling down all around him. He turned toward the rumbling sound and saw an enormous creature crash through the brick warehouse walls. Two horns jutted out of its narrow, gray head. An ugly mane snaked down its back to its tail. And its claws were destroying everything in sight. It was the Lizzinator.

"Power Rangers...I will destroy the puny Power Rangers," the Lizzinator roared. "I must find the Power Rangers!" Then the monster broke through another wall and left the building.

"Oh, man," Jason cried with

amazement. "It's morphin time!"

The air crackled with electricity as Jason raised his Power Morpher to the sky. Just as Zordon had taught him, he called upon the spirit of an ancient dinosaur.

"Tyrannosaurus!" cried Jason. In a flash, Jason morphed into a Power Ranger! Now he stood in his sleek red jumpsuit and helmet. He was a powerful protector—the Red Ranger.

Jason ran into the street and spotted the monster lumbering over to a parked car.

"Ha-ha-ha! A toy to play with," grunted the Lizzinator. It lifted the car and hurled it across the road—straight at Jason. "Take that!" it roared.

Jason stumbled back, dodging the Lizzinator's jumbo toy. The Lizzinator laughed loudly.

"You wanna play rough, tough guy?" Jason asked. He whisked out his Power Sword and charged at the horrible creature. But the blows just glanced off the Lizzinator's rock-hard skin.

"You are no match for me," joked the Lizzinator, pinning Jason to the overturned car. "My super strength will crush you."

"Wanna bet?" challenged Jason. "You're just an overgrown creepy crawler."

The Red Ranger wriggled free

and charged the Lizzinator again. This time the Lizzinator scooped Jason up and held him high over its head.

"Now I will crush your puny human body!"

As Jason struggled to free himself from the iron grip of the monster's claws, the Lizzinator laughed hideously. Then it hurled Jason through the air. The Red Ranger landed hard against a row of metal garbage cans.

"This is too easy," cackled the Lizzinator. "I want to fight all the puny Power Rangers at once. I want a good challenge for my super strength! Don't worry, I'll be back."

Then the Lizzinator vanished in a flash of purple light.

Jason pulled himself to his feet and spoke into the communicator on his wrist.

"Zordon, this is Jason. We've got major trouble on Earth."

Zordon's voice came through clearly. "Teleport to the Command Center at once!"

When Jason arrived at the Command Center, the other Power Rangers were waiting there for him.

"Rita's taken Kelly," Kimberly explained. "We've got to do something—fast."

"Oh, no!" Jason groaned.

"That's not all—Rita's let loose another monster."

Behind them, a pale image in a wavering column of green light spoke. It was Zordon. His low voice echoed through the room.

"Rita's new monster is called the Lizzinator. Rangers, its power is far superior to anything we've ever seen before."

"I'll say," said Jason. "I already had a run-in with it, and I was way outmatched."

"Well, what if we combine our powers?" said Billy thoughtfully. "Together we can beat this power lizard."

"I'm afraid even the six of you together may be no match for the

37

Lizzinator," Zordon replied.

"Wow! It's that powerful?" Trini gasped.

"Aye-yi-yi-yi-yi!" exclaimed Alpha 5, the robot who ran the Command Center. "We've got trouble." The lights on Alpha's metal head flashed on and off.

"Alpha, show Billy the computer reading on this new monster," Zordon instructed.

Alpha zipped to the huge control panel, picked up a minicomputer, and handed it to Billy.

Billy's blue eyes looked troubled behind his glasses as he read the tiny screen. "The Lizzinator's skin is made of super metals from another galaxy. These metals are

"The monster is tearing apart another building. Soon there'll be nothing left on Earth."

"No way, Alpha. We're on it!" Zack exclaimed.

"Alpha, while we're gone, please try to find out where Rita has taken Kelly!" Kimberly begged.

"Okay, guys," Jason said. "It's morphin time!"

"Dragon!" cried Tommy, calling on the fearsome creature that was his special spirit.

"Mastodon!" cried Zack.

"Pterodactyl!" cried Kimberly.

"Triceratops!" cried Billy.

"Saber-toothed Tiger!" cried Trini.

"Tyrannosaurus!" cried Jason.

In a flash, the six teens from Angel Grove morphed into— Power Rangers! Kimberly's outfit was bright pink. Trini's was yellow. Billy's was blue. Tommy's was green. Jason wore red, and Zack wore black.

"Power Rangers!" they shouted and vanished. An instant later they reappeared on a cliff just above the Lizzinator.

"Another toy to play with," grunted the monster, as it bounded toward a parked car.

"Hold it right there, lizard-breath," Jason commanded.

"Ah! All the Power Rangers are here!" The Lizzinator's eyes lit up. "Finally, a challenge!"

The evil reptile advanced toward the six Power Rangers. Then it fired its laser eyes right at them. The Power Rangers cartwheeled out of the lasers' path. But when they landed, they saw they had company—the Putty Patrol!

"Ha-ha-ha-ha!" laughed the Lizzinator. "Some of my friends want to say 'hi'!"

The Putties surrounded the Power Rangers. "Hit it!" shouted Trini, the Yellow Ranger.

"Ki-yaaah!" Zack shouted as he side kicked the Putty nearest him.

Then the Red Ranger spotted the Lizzinator stomping back

toward the parked car.

"Oh, no you don't," yelled Jason. He somersaulted through the air into the car. But a Putty was already inside, and it shoved Jason hard—right out the door.

The Putty scooted behind the wheel and started the engine. Jason leaped on top of the car's roof. He could barely hold on as he was tossed back and forth. The Putty was driving straight for a cliff while the Lizzinator hit the car with fireball after fireball.

As the car plunged off the edge of the cliff, the Putty vanished. Jason leaped from the roof. He tumbled down a steep hill and landed safely in the valley below.

But the Lizzinator was waiting for him.

"Nice landing, Red Ranger," the Lizzinator snorted. "Watch me land this." Without another word, the Lizzinator lifted an enormous boulder and hurled it at Jason. He dodged, but the huge rock slammed hard into his shoulder.

The Lizzinator hoisted another rock and threw it. But this time, Tommy, the Green Ranger, flipped in front of it. With a powerful karate kick, he sent the rock flying—right back at the Lizzinator.

"You all right, buddy?" Tommy asked Jason, keeping his eyes glued to the Lizzinator.

"I'm okay," answered Jason.

But when he tried to stand up, he fell to his knees in pain.

"It's my shoulder," Jason winced. "I don't think I'll be able to help you."

Tommy glanced up the hill, hoping for Power Ranger backup. But it looked as though the Putties were still giving the others a tough fight.

Now it was up to Tommy to save them both—and the Lizzinator was headed straight toward him!

CHAPTER 7

Meanwhile, on the moon, Kelly sat shivering in Rita's hidden cave. She stayed as far away as possible from her kidnappers, Squatt and Baboo, who were bragging to each other.

"I bet Rita will give us a big reward," said Baboo. "It isn't too often that we do something right."

"Yeah," replied Squatt. "I hope it's food." At the thought of eating, Squatt's lips stretched into a big ugly smile.

While the two goons dreamed about filling their bellies, Kelly's eyes searched the cave. She had found the cave opening, but she was too scared to make a move toward it.

Then Kelly remembered what Kimberly had told her. *Never give up. Believe in yourself and you can do whatever you want.*

Kelly thought about those words. Then she took a deep breath and walked over to Squatt and Baboo. She had a plan.

"Hey guys," she said, "want to learn some cheers?"

While Kelly put her plan into action, the Lizzinator and the Green Ranger battled on. The Green Ranger was winning! And the other Power Rangers had just knocked all the Putties to the ground.

"No! No! No!" Rita screeched from her balcony on the moon. She was watching the fight through her telescope. "Those power brats will not win this time. Not with the surprise I'm going to give them."

Rita rushed to the edge of the balcony. She raised her magic staff into the air.

"Make my Lizzinator grow!" Rita screamed. Then she hurled her staff toward Earth. Bolts of lightning shot out of the staff as it stabbed into the Earth. They snaked out and wrapped around the Lizzinator.

Tommy and the Power Rangers watched in horror as the lizard monster grew bigger and bigger and bigger.

"Now I will crush you," the Lizzinator roared.

Tommy called for the power of the Dragonzord to help him fight. Instantly, he was transported inside the huge dragon robot.

"Finally a playmate my size! I

think I'll rip it to pieces." The Lizzinator cackled and lunged at the Dragonzord. It seized the Zord by the tail and swung it around and around. Then the monster slammed the Dragonzord to the ground.

"Dragonzord's in trouble," shouted the Red Ranger. "We need Dinozord Power!"

The other Power Rangers quickly called out their dinosaurs' names. "Tyrannosaurus!" "Pterodactyl!" "Mastodon!" "Saber-toothed Tiger!" "Triceratops!"

The ground trembled with the distant sound of the dinosaur robots awakening.

Tyrannosaurus erupted from a

steaming crack in the ground.

Mastodon broke through its cage of ice.

Triceratops charged across a scorching desert.

Saber-toothed Tiger leaped through a twisted jungle.

Pterodactyl erupted from the fires of a volcano.

Just as the Dragonzord had instantly responded to Tommy's call for help, the Dinozords raced like the wind to answer the other Power Rangers.

Then two Zords locked into a third, *Clunk! Clang!* and became legs. Two more Zords locked in, *Clang! Thunk!* and formed arms.

The mighty head rose from its

chest. Its helmet swung open and locked into place. Its shield clanged into its chest.

In moments, the Dinozords locked together to become the mighty Megazord!

Jason and the other Power Rangers teleported to the control room right behind the Megazord's flashing eyes. "Okay. It's time to rock," the Red Ranger said.

"Let's take this guy down," Zack, the Black Ranger, yelled.

"All systems are go," Billy added. "We're fully operational."

"Are you ready, lizard-breath?" Trini, the Yellow Ranger, shouted.

"Lizzinator, you're about to get scaled!" cried Kimberly.

"You ready, Tommy?" Jason shouted to the Green Ranger inside the Dragonzord.

"You bet!" the Green Ranger answered.

The ground shook as Megazord and Dragonzord thundered toward the huge monster.

"Two of you?" Lizzinator grumbled. "No problem. Let's see how you like my super-stinky breath!" The Lizzinator blew a gust of smoke from its mouth that exploded all around the Zords.

"I am indestructible," roared the Lizzinator. "And now I will carry out Queen Rita's orders. I will destroy you both!"

"Jason! Tommy!" Billy called.

"Our only chance to penetrate the super metal skin is to combine the Megazord and Dragonzord power beams."

"Let's do it!" Jason and Tommy shouted. Instantly, the two Zords united to form—Ultrazord Power! The Ultrazord unleashed its power beams. They blasted the Lizzinator right in the stomach. The force was so powerful that the Lizzinator exploded—and vaporized into nothing.

"We did it!" shouted Trini. "We saved the Earth!"

As the Power Rangers cheered, Rita watched from her balcony. She was so mad that she was pulling her hair out.

"I absolutely can't stand you, Power Rangers," she cried, waving an angry fist.

Back on Earth, the Power Rangers' wrist communicators beeped and Zordon's deep voice boomed through. "Good work, Power Rangers," he said. "And good news: Alpha has located Kimberly's cousin. As soon as we have the exact spot, we'll let you know. Stand by and be ready for transport."

Meanwhile, in the cave, Baboo and Squatt had their eyes fixed on Kelly. Her escape plan was working! The two goons wanted to learn cheers.

"Here we go," Kelly said. "Just copy me." Then she began.

"Rita! Rita! She's your leader. But the Power Rangers always beat her!"

As Kelly performed several complicated jumps and spins, Squatt and Baboo tried to follow. Each time Kelly repeated the cheer, she moved faster and shouted louder.

Soon Baboo and Squatt were twirling around, falling all over each other, and tripping over their own feet. They were so dizzy that they were certain their heads would spin right off their shoulders.

"Oooooh, my stomach," wailed

Baboo. "I'm going to be sick."

"I don't feel so good, either," moaned Squatt.

Kelly kept cheering louder and louder. Her voice echoed through the cave. Baboo and Squatt held their hands over their ears.

"Stop!" shouted Squatt. "Make her stop!" he ordered Baboo.

"You make her stop! It was your idea to learn this in the first place, you big blue baboon!" Baboo shouted back.

"I can't take her screams," shouted Squatt.

"I'm getting out of here," Baboo cried.

"Wait for me," Squatt shouted.

With that, the two goons vanished into space—just as the Power Rangers landed in the cave. Kimberly, the Pink Ranger, rushed over to Kelly.

"Wow," said Kelly. "The Power Rangers!"

"Kelly," said the Pink Ranger, "your cousin Kimberly sent us to find you. She's very worried about you. Are you hurt?" Nobody, not even Kimberly's cousin, was allowed to know the Power Rangers' true identities.

"No, I'm not hurt," said Kelly. "And I wasn't really scared. I just remembered the advice that Kimberly gave me. She said if I believe in myself, I can do anything."

"Sounds like good advice to me," the Green Ranger said, giving the Pink Ranger a knowing nod.

"I can't wait to go home and tell Kimberly I got rid of the bad guys on my own. *And* I got to meet the Power Rangers! This is so cool!"

"Well, then. Let's rock and roll home!" the Black Ranger shouted.

The Pink Ranger took hold of Kelly's hand and said, "Hold on tight."

In a flash, the Power Rangers and Kelly teleported back to the Angel Grove Youth Center.

"Wow, that was awesome," Kelly exclaimed. "Thanks, Power Rangers." Then she dashed inside the gym, where cheerleader tryouts were about to begin.

"Good luck!" the Power Rangers shouted after her. Then they stepped behind some tall bushes where no one could see them. A few moments later, six teenagers dressed in ordinary clothes stepped out from behind the shrubs.

Kimberly, Trini, Billy, Jason, Tommy, and Zack were back to their regular selves—until the next time evil forces threatened the Earth again.

The six teens entered the gym just as Kelly was called to her try-out. They watched as she performed a perfect routine. It was so good, it blew everyone away!

"She did it! She did it!" everyone shouted.

The cheers for Kelly were so loud, she almost didn't hear the coach say, "Congratulations, Kelly. You made the team!"